CR

Somerset County Library System
100 Collins Street
Crisfield, MD 21817
CRISFIELD BRANCH

Freshwater Fish
Sturgeon

Leo Statts

Launch!
An Imprint of Abdo Zoom
abdopublishing.com

abdopublishing.com

Published by Abdo Zoom, a division of ABDO, PO Box 398166, Minneapolis, Minnesota 55439.
Copyright © 2019 by Abdo Consulting Group, Inc. International copyrights reserved in all countries.
No part of this book may be reproduced in any form without written permission from the publisher.
Launch!™ is a trademark and logo of Abdo Zoom.

Printed in the United States of America, North Mankato, Minnesota.

052018
092018

Photo Credits: Alamy, AP Images, Engbretson Underwater Photography, iStock, Seapics.com, Shutterstock

Production Contributors: Kenny Abdo, Jennie Forsberg, Grace Hansen, John Hansen

Design Contributors: Dorothy Toth, Neil Klinepier

Library of Congress Control Number: 2017960513

Publisher's Cataloging-in-Publication Data

Names: Statts, Leo, author.

Title: Sturgeon / by Leo Statts.

Description: Minneapolis, Minnesota : Abdo Zoom, 2019. | Series: Freshwater fish |
    Includes online resources and index.

Identifiers: ISBN 9781532122910 (lib.bdg.) | ISBN 9781532123894 (ebook) |
    ISBN 9781532124389 (Read-to-me ebook)

Subjects: LCSH: Lake sturgeon--Juvenile literature. | Freshwater fishes--Juvenile literature. |
    Paddlefish--Juvenile literature. | Fishes--Juvenile literature.

Classification: DDC 597.42--dc23

Table of Contents

Sturgeon 4

Body.. 6

Habitat 10

Food 14

Life Cycle 18

Quick Stats... 20

Glossary.. 22

Online Resources...................... 23

Index 24

Sturgeon

Sturgeon have been around for 135 million years. There are many different **species**.

They come in different colors and sizes.

Body

Sturgeon are covered in **scutes**. It is like armor. It protects the fish.

Sturgeon have **barbels** that look like whiskers. They have rounded **snouts** and no teeth.

Habitat

Sturgeon can live in salt water and **fresh water**.

They are found in rivers and lakes.

Sturgeon often live near **coasts**.

Food

Sturgeon are **omnivores**.

They eat fish, crayfish, and clams. They hunt at the bottom of the sea or river.

They swallow their food whole.

Life Cycle

Sturgeon start out as eggs. It takes 20 years for a sturgeon to be full grown.

Scientists believe sturgeon can live for more than 100 years.

Average Weight

A beluga sturgeon weighs more than a refrigerator.

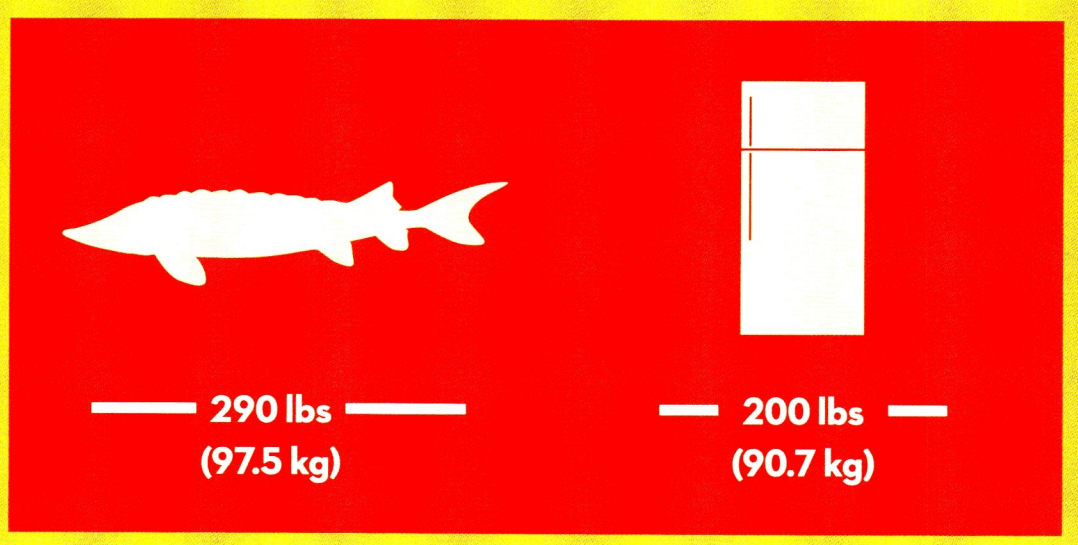

290 lbs (97.5 kg)

200 lbs (90.7 kg)

Average Weight

A shovelnose sturgeon weighs more than a textbook.

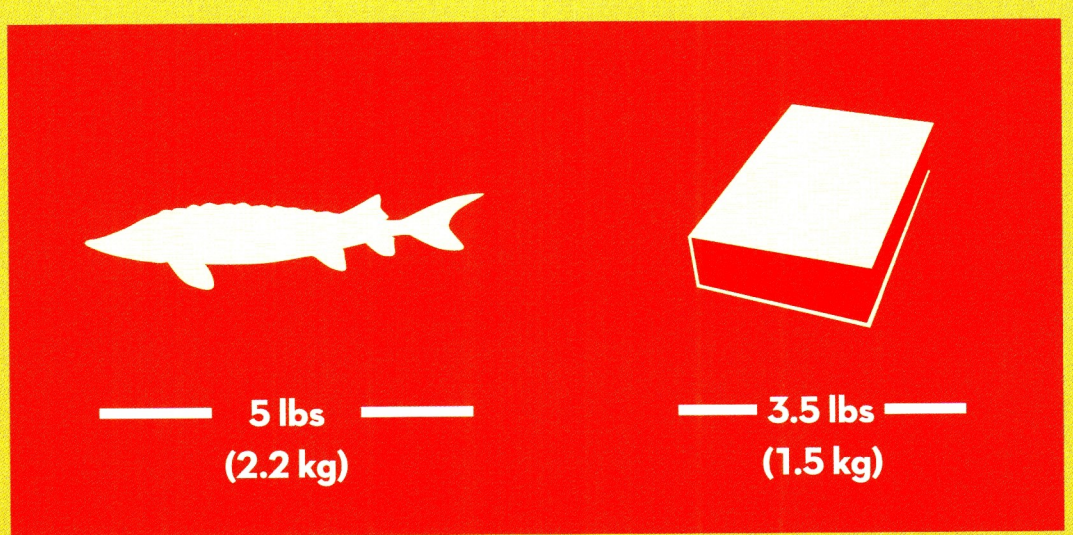

5 lbs (2.2 kg)

3.5 lbs (1.5 kg)

Glossary

barbel – a whisker-like organ found near the mouths of sturgeons that are used to find food.

coast – the land near a body of water.

fresh water – water that does not have salt in it like oceans do.

omnivore – an animal that eats both plants and animals.

scute – a bony plate that covers a sturgeon's body.

snout – the part of the face that sticks out, including the nose and mouth.

species – living things that are very much alike.

Online Resources

For more information on sturgeon, please visit **abdobooklinks.com**

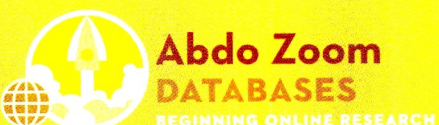

Learn even more with the Abdo Zoom Animals database. Visit **abdozoom.com** today!

Index

barbel 8

color 5

eggs 18

food 14, 15, 16

fresh water 10, 12, 15

habitat 10, 12, 13

lifespan 19

salt water 10, 13, 15

size 5

skin 6

species 4, 5